The Berenstain

VISIT Grizzlyland

Magical wonders
will be at your command
when you visit a place
known as Grizzlyland!

Mike Berenstain

Based on the characters created by
Stan and Jan Berenstain

HARPER FESTIVAL
An Imprint of HarperCollins*Publishers*

 For information address HarperCollins Children's Books, a division of HarperCollins Publishers, 195 Broadway, New York, NY 10007.
www.harpercollinschildrens.com
Library of Congress Control Number: 2017951267
ISBN 978-0-06-265463-2
20 21 22 23 SCP 10 9 8 7 6 5 ❖ First Edition

The Bear family was going on a very special trip, one they had been planning for a long, long time. Brother, Sister, and Honey were so excited they could hardly breathe.

They were on their way, flying in a great silver airliner, to that most magical spot in all of Bear Country—the famous theme park Grizzlyland!

At last the plane touched down. Everyone on board cheered and clapped.

"Yay!" cried the cubs. "We're here!"

Papa was just as excited as the cubs.

"I can hardly wait to go on the Pirates of the Bearibbean ride!" he said. Papa was really into Pirates of the Bearibbean.

They climbed aboard a shiny Grizzlyland bus that whisked them right to their hotel.

The hotel was like a theme park in itself. A jungle of tropical trees grew in the lobby. Brightly colored parrots perched in the branches.

"Hello!" said Sister to a big blue one.

"Heroh!" it said back.

After they checked out the view from their room's balcony, the family was ready to hit the park. They were eager to try out all the exciting rides.

A special train called a monorail took them from the hotel to the park. Honey thought the monorail was one of the rides.

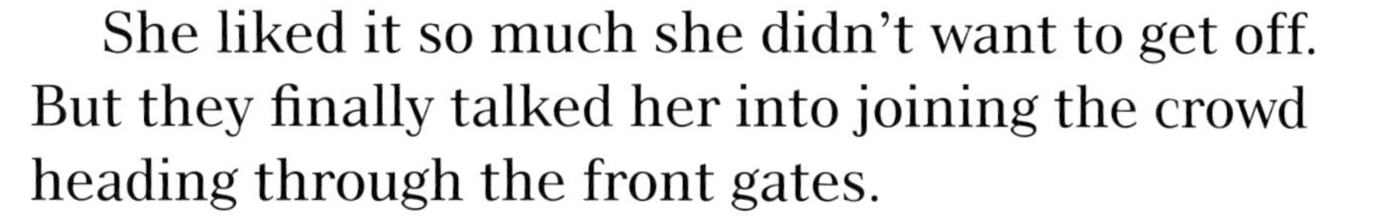

She liked it so much she didn't want to get off. But they finally talked her into joining the crowd heading through the front gates.

They emerged into a wonderful world of the imagination. There were old-fashioned buildings and old-fashioned trolleys. A band dressed in old-fashioned costumes played quaint old tunes.

And there were famous characters to meet—the ones they knew so well from movies and TV: Harry Hamster and Charlie Chicken, Gloria Gopher and Abelard Aardvark, the lovely Princess Petunia and handsome Prince Percival. You could even get your picture taken with them.

MAIN ST.
PHOTOS HERE

And now it was time for the rides.

"How about Pirates of the Bearibbean?" suggested Papa.

"Sounds good," said Sister. "But Space Grizzlies is right here. Let's do that first."

It was a roller coaster that zipped wildly around Grizzly Galaxy. It went up and down and looped the loop. Space Grizzlies popped out from behind planets as the cubs zapped them with their space zappers.

"Woooah . . . !" moaned Papa, his head spinning.

EXIT
Spinning Honey Pots
HONEY
HONEY

"That was okay for starters," said Brother when it was over. "Let's look for something more exciting."

"How about Pirates of the Bearibbean?" asked Papa hopefully.

"Sure!" said Sister. "But the Spinning Honey Pots are next."

They sat in big honey pots that spun around and around and around. The cubs laughed and screamed.

"Woooah . . . !" moaned Papa, getting dizzy.

"That was fine—a little tame," said Brother. "What's next?"

"How about Pirates of the Bearibbean?" asked Papa shakily.

"No problem," said Sister. "But I'm hungry. How about lunch?"

They stopped at a 1950s-style Burger Bear. They were served by waitresses on roller skates. They had milkshakes, triple honey-burgers, and French fries.

"Woooah . . . !" said Papa, feeling a little sick.

"That hit the spot," said Brother, licking his lips. "Now, another ride."
"How about Pirates of the Bearibbean?" asked Papa faintly.
"Sure thing," said Sister. "But Sploosh Mountain is on our way."
They got into a hollow log floating in a trough.

It climbed up and up and up. It wound in and about an old mining camp. Then, it went down and down and down! They went "SPLOOOSH!" into a pool at the bottom.

"Woooah . . . !" moaned Papa, getting wet.

"That was pretty good," admitted Brother. "Now what?"
"How about . . ." Papa began weakly.
"Pirates of the Bearibbean!" they all said together.
"Look, Papa, look!" said Mama. "We're here!"
Sure enough, the Pirates of the Bearibbean ride rose before them. It looked like a mysterious old fortress. They went inside.

There were cannons and barrels of gunpowder. There were dungeons and flaring torches. They climbed into a pirate boat that floated off into darkness. A cold wind blew in their faces. A spooky voice called, “Beware! Beware!”

Suddenly, they came to a harbor where a battle was going on. A pirate ship fired its cannon at a town's walls. The town fired back. Cannonballs splashed all around them. It was very exciting!

"Oh boy! Oh boy!" said Papa, bouncing up and down in his seat.

"Papa, sit down!" said Mama. "You're rocking the boat!"

When the ride was over, they came out, blinking, into the bright sunlight.

"That was *soooo* cool!" said Papa. "Let's do it again!"

The whole family laughed.

"How about Pirates of the Bearibbean?" they said as they led a very happy Papa Bear back inside.